# Ms. Broomstick's School for Witches

by Jana Dillon

illustrated by Rebecca McKillip Thornburgh

Troll

To my three wonderful sisters,
Jeannie, Susie, and Irene
—with love, Jana

For Bob and Zoë Alley,
friends wise and magical
—Rebecca

When the sun sets, it's time for class to begin at Ms. Broomstick's School. During the day, it is a regular school. But when night falls, Ms. Broomstick waves her wand and transforms the building into a perfect school for young witches.

The students are filing in. Pandora is last in line. She is almost late—again!

"Good evening, little witches," says Ms. Broomstick. "Tonight we will learn some exciting lessons. I know you will all be careful listeners. You are wonderful students."

Now that is a good way to warm the hearts of the little witches on this crisp October evening!

"Which little witch remembers which lesson is first?" Ms. Broomstick asks.

"I do!" Pandora calls out. "We learn to ride our brooms!"

Pandora runs to the broom corner, and the other little witches hurry along behind her. Now she is first in line, not last.

The little witches are new at flying. Notice how they fly their broomsticks close to the ground. They don't want to fall too far.

"Great bats and cats!" cries Ms. Broomstick.
Pandora is doing a handstand on her broom.
"Please sit on the broom, Pandora," Ms. Broomstick
says sternly. "Remember what I said about safety?"

Crash!

Oh, my. Poor little witch!

"Are you okay, dear?" Ms. Broomstick helps Pandora up. "Don't worry, pumpkin. Someday you will be a topflight witch. Just listen to *all* the directions before you start."

Ms. Broomstick leads the little witches to the Black Cat Room. "It's kitten time," the teacher says. "You must train your very own black kitten to be a good—no!—a *great* witch's cat."

The students pet and play with their kittens. The kittens love their little witches.

Pandora's kitten teases her by playing hide-and-seek.

"Pandora," says Ms. Broomstick, "the kitten is *your* pet—you are not the kitten's pet."

Just like little witches, kittens are not born knowing how to use magic. The students must teach them. Today the kittens are learning to change into baby ravens.

"Excellent, excellent," says Ms. Broomstick. "But wait, what is that terrible smell?"

"It's us, Ms. Broomstick," wails Pandora. "My kitten turned into a skunk!"

Ms. Broomstick smiles and shakes her head. "Remember to listen to *all* the directions before you begin, Pandora."

She shows Pandora how to train her kitten. Soon Pandora's kitten turns into a fluffy raven chick and back again.

Next, the students head to the Witches' Kitchen. "All little witches must learn to stew a fine cauldron of witch's brew," says Ms. Broomstick.

She hands out the ingredients: a clump of cobwebs, a handful of snake tongues, a pinch of toad warts, an armload of bat fur, a bucket of alligator armpits, and, of course, one eye of newt each.

Ms. Broomstick and the students chant:

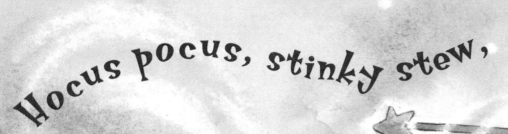

Hocus pocus, stinky stew,

Change into a witch's brew.

"I can make my brew bubble like my mother's brew," says Pandora.

"Your mother's brew is boiling hot," Ms. Broomstick says. "Our school brew is safely cold."

"It will be safe!" says Pandora. "I brought bubble bath to school!"

"Wait, Pandora!" cries Ms. Broomstick. "Don't open that box!"

Too late! Bubbles cover Pandora, the kittens, and all the other little witches, too!

"Bubble trouble!" says Ms. Broomstick. "Bubble, bubble, toil and trouble. Pandora, when will you learn to listen to directions?"

The little witch's shoulders slump.

Ms. Broomstick takes pity on her. "It's all right, dear. Let's just clean up."

With the help of Ms. Broomstick's magic wand, the kitchen is tidy in no time at all.

"Now we'll learn how to carve jack-o'-lanterns," Ms. Broomstick announces.

"Make the eyes and nose the shape of triangles," she tells the class. "Is everyone paying attention? Pandora? Are you listening?"

Pandora loves the squishy pumpkin pulp. She squeezes it between her hands until it squirts out.

**Splat!**

Oh, no! Ms. Broomstick is covered with pulp. "Great bats and pointed hats!" she cries.

"I'm sorry, Ms. Broomstick!" wails Pandora.

"Don't worry, Pandora, I can wipe it off," says Ms. Broomstick. "But please, please listen to my directions!"

Once the jack-o'-lanterns have been carved, it is snack time. *Mmm, mmm*! The little witches love their fried pumpkin seeds.

The other witches giggle at Pandora. She is throwing the seeds in the air and catching them in her mouth.

Ms. Broomstick sighs. "Fiddlesticks and broomsticks!" she says to herself. Then she calls out, "Class, it's time for recess."

Pandora organizes a new game called Bobbing for Toads.
The little witches shriek and laugh.

"What is going on?" asks Ms. Broomstick.

"Pandora won!" shout the students.

"Congratulations, Pandora," says Ms. Broomstick. She rolls her eyes. "Now spit out that toad and lead your friends to the sink. Gargle, everyone!"

Ms. Broomstick notices the time. "My stars!" she says. "It's already eleven o'clock. At midnight it will be the witching hour. That's when every little witch should be home with her family, casting spells or mixing magic brews."

Ms. Broomstick passes out sponges. "Let's chant our clean-up spell."

Icky, acky, dirty grunge!
Clean it quickly, magic sponge!

**Oh, dear!**

Pandora's sponge is out of control. She needs Ms. Broomstick's help—again!

"Now tuck in your kittens," says Ms. Broomstick.

The tiny black cats are sleepy at the end of the busy night.

The little witches gently carry their kittens to bed. But Pandora still wants to play.

"Calm down, Pandora," says Ms. Broomstick. "You'll get your kitten all wound up."

"Nighty-night, little kitty," says Pandora. She runs to say good-bye to the toads in the tub—and forgets to shut the kittens' gate.

"Fetch your jack-o'-lanterns and line up to go home, students," says Ms. Broomstick.

Pandora turns quickly to listen to Ms. Broomstick's directions—and bumps into the shelf. ⌇Bang!⌇

The tub of toads falls. Hop, hop! Squeak, squeak! Toads are everywhere!

**Meow!** The kittens run out to chase the toads.
"Thunderation!" cries Ms. Broomstick.
"What's going on? Why, it's Pandora again!"

Ms. Broomstick quickly takes charge. "Hurry, little witches!" she calls. "Catch your kittens!"

The tiny witches chase the kittens. The kittens chase the toads. The toads hop and leap. Little witches shout, "Here, kitty, kitty!" Kittens hiss and meow. Toads ribbit.

Ms. Broomstick can't believe the wild classroom.

She waves her wand.

Suddenly the toads are in the tub.
Each kitten stops. The little witches pause,
surprised, and look at Ms. Broomstick.

"Kittens to bed!" she orders.

The students quietly carry their kittens back
to bed. This time, Pandora closes the gate.

Ms. Broomstick slumps into a chair as the little witches line up to go home with their jack-o'-lanterns.

Wait. What's this? Pandora is out of line. She comes over to her teacher.

"Ms. Broomstick?" she asks in a small, worried voice. "Ms. Broomstick?"

"Yes, Pandora?"

"Ms. Broomstick, was I any trouble for you tonight?"

Ms. Broomstick leans over and says to the tiny witch,
"Sweet Pandora, you fill our school night with surprises."
"I love you, Ms. Broomstick," says Pandora, beaming with joy.
"And I promise to be full of surprises tomorrow. Bye!"